Brander Matthews

This Picture and That

A comedy

Brander Matthews

This Picture and That
A comedy

ISBN/EAN: 9783744781527

Printed in Europe, USA, Canada, Australia, Japan

Cover: Foto ©Andreas Hilbeck / pixelio.de

More available books at **www.hansebooks.com**

"DASHING DICK WILLOUGHBY"

THIS PICTURE AND THAT

A Comedy

BY

BRANDER MATTHEWS

ILLUSTRATED

NEW YORK

HARPER & BROTHERS PUBLISHERS

1894

Harper's "Black and White" Series

Illustrated. 32mo, Cloth, 50 cents each.

PUBLISHED BY HARPER & BROTHERS, NEW YORK

For sale by all booksellers, or will be sent by the publishers, postage prepaid, on receipt of price.

NOTE

[*This comedy was acted at the Lyceum Theatre in New York in 1887, with Miss Mathilde Madison as* Mrs. Willoughby, *and with Mr. Henry Miller as* Major John Strong. *During the same season my friend Mr. Bronson Howard produced his vigorous drama of American life and character, "The Henrietta"; and on his programme he gave credit to the author of "Vanity Fair" for one situation of his new play. This drew my attention to the fact that I, too, had borrowed this same situation of Thackeray's for the present comedy. It was a clever school-boy, I think, and not a dull one, who defined a "plagiarist" as "a writer of plays." My plagiarism (if so it must be called) was perhaps the less heinous for being wholly unconscious — as Thackeray himself had probably forgotten that Leatherstocking died saying "Here!" a score of years before Colonel Newcome drew himself up on his death-bed and answered to the roll-call, "Adsum!"*]

LIST OF ILLUSTRATIONS

THIS PICTURE AND THAT

CAST OF CHARACTERS

———

Mrs. WILLOUGHBY.

Major JOHN STRONG, U.S.V.

Dr. DOULTON, formerly surgeon U.S.A.

A HALL-BOY of the Hotel.

———

SCENE :—Mrs. Willoughby's parlor in the Fifth Avenue Hotel, New York.

———

TIME :—An evening in the spring of 1864.

I

THE time is the evening of a day in the
spring of 1864, and the scene is a parlor of
the Fifth Avenue Hotel. The parlor is like
most other hotel parlors. There is a mantel-piece on one side of it, separating two
windows which look out on Madison Square.
On the opposite side is a desk ; and a little
beyond this is the door leading into Mrs.
Willoughby's bedroom. The door at the
back of the parlor opens into the hall of the
hotel. There is a sofa before the fireplace.
There is an easel near one of the windows,
empty, but with a silk flag thrown over it
carelessly. In one of the upper corners
stands a piano.

Mrs. Willoughby is seated at her piano,
playing one after another of a collection of
war-songs: "Tramp, Tramp, Tramp, the

2

Boys are Marching," "The Battle-cry of Freedom," and at last "Johnny Comes Marching Home." Then she plays more slowly, until at last she stops and speaks:

"And some poor fellows do not come marching home. I do wish Major Strong had not to go back to the war again. I shall miss him very much. It is strange how a woman can get to know a man in a few short months. This time last year I had never heard of Major Strong; and last summer, when I read the news of the battle of Gettysburg, I could have seen his name in the list of the wounded without any other emotion than the vague pity a woman feels for all those who have suffered while doing their duty. And now I hate the very idea of his going back into danger. [*She turns to the piano again and plays the same tune softly.*] And his name is John, too! I won't believe that anything can happen to him; this Johnny will come marching home again! [*She stops playing once more.*] After all, what is it to me whether he goes or comes—whether he lives or dies? I'm not in love with the man! He hasn't asked me to marry him—yet. And I wouldn't if he did! [*She turns to piano and plays the " Old Folks at Home" very gently.*] But I can confess that I like Major Strong very much—very much indeed. Why shouldn't I be fond of him? He is kind, and considerate, and attentive. I'm sure I shall miss him when he is gone. And this is his last evening, and he is coming to bid me good-bye."

[*As she is playing softly and dreamily, a knock is heard. She jumps up and runs to the door of her own room.*

" Perhaps that is he now! And I am not fit to be seen. Come in !"

[*A* hall-boy *appears in the doorway.*

The hall-boy: "Some flowers for you, mum, and a letter."

Mrs. Willoughby: "Put them on the table."

The hall-boy: "All right, mum."

[*He places a bunch of flowers and a letter on the parlor table, and is going back to the door as* Mrs. Willoughby *checks him with a sudden exclamation.*

Mrs. Willoughby: "Oh! Just ask at the office if a picture has not been sent for me. I'm expecting a portrait this evening, and it ought to be here now."

The hall-boy: "I'll look it up, mum."

[*Then he disappears, closing the door after him.*

Mrs. Willoughby (*going to the table*): "Roses and lilies of the valley—my favorite flowers—they are from the Major, I'm sure. [*She takes up the flowers and sees the card attached.*] Here's his card—P.P.C. I know I shall miss him ever so much! [*She arranges the flowers in a vase on the table.*] And he has added forget-me-nots, too. I don't think I am likely to forget him, however far away he may go. I don't know how I should ever have lived through the winter without him. A widow has a hard time all by herself unless some one takes pity on her. How well those forget-me-nots set off the roses and lilies of the valley !"

[*As she moves away to get a better look at the flowers, the letter is brushed off the table and falls to the floor.*

"My letter! I wonder now who wrote
it? [*She picks it up.*] It's from Daisy Brown,
I declare."

> [*She opens the envelope, throwing it care-
> lessly on the table, and then begins to
> read the letter.*

"CHICAGO, *May* 1st, 1864.

"'MY DARLING MARY,'—My darling Mary
—and she hasn't written me for nearly six
months. [*Reading again.*] 'I should have
answered your last letter long ago, if I hadn't
been so busy settling up the accounts of our
Sanitary Fair. The General—you know that
my husband has just been brevetted a brig-
adier.' I didn't know it—and I was wonder-
ing what had moved her to write to me all
of a sudden; I see now that she wanted to
break the news gently. [*Reading.*] 'The
General wants to know if we are to congratulate you on your engagement to Captain
Strong.' Now I wonder what could have
put such a silly idea into their heads?
[*Reading.*] 'We have heard the rumor

from several sources.' I wish people in Chicago would find something to talk about. I'd like it better if they would attend to their own divorces, and just let our marriages alone. [*Reading.*] 'The General says that if you are engaged, he can congratulate you heartily ; he has the highest opinion of Captain Strong.' I suppose Captain Strong ought to feel very much complimented by General Brown's praise. [*Reading.*] 'You know the General commanded the brigade at Gettysburg when Captain Strong was wounded, and so he knows all about him.' "

[Mrs. Willoughby *pauses in her reading for a moment.*] "I wonder how Daisy Brown would like me to write her patronizing praise of the General, as she calls him ! [*Then she took up the letter again.*] 'I trust you will excuse my frankness, darling Mary, when I say I hope you will take Captain Strong. You know I never approved of your first husband.' Well, I like that—

and she did all she could to catch him for herself. That's the reason I asked her to be a bridesmaid."

[Mrs. Willoughby *continues reading, but with a growing indignation.*] "'The General calls him "a man you can tie to," as we say here in the West. He is just the husband you need to anchor your vagrant fancies, for you know you are inclined to be sentimental, not to say flighty.' Well, Daisy Brown, this is cool! But I'll make it hot for you when you get my answer. I wonder what she will dare to say next. [*Reading.*] 'What is perhaps Captain Strong's chief recommendation is that he is the exact opposite of the late Colonel Willoughby, whom you did not really love, although you are still trying to persuade yourself that you did. To wear mourning for a man two years after he is dead is indelicate, and I do hope you have given it up. You were dazzled by Dick Willoughby's good looks, and by his dashing ways;

but I don't believe you cared any more for him than he did for you—and that was little enough. He married you for your money, and it is lucky for you he did not live to spend it all.' "

Mrs. Willoughby (*rising rapidly from her chair*): "This is really too much! Of course poor Dick was extravagant, and he hadn't any money of his own, but he was very fond of me. She speaks of him as if he were a mere fortune-hunter, and she writes to me as if I were a silly school-girl. [*Walking across the room to a desk near the window.*] I wish I could return her letter unread! At least, I'll send it back, and beg her not to intrude on me again with her advice and her boasting! If I said all I wanted to say I should have to use red ink and a red-hot pen. I wish I could have her here for five minutes. I think I could use language that would astonish her—even though she does live in Chicago. How shall I begin? [*She takes up her pen and writes.*] 'Madam, I

3

take pleasure in returning your most im-
pertinent letter [*a knock is heard at the
door*], and I forbid your writing me again.'
There! I wonder how she will like that."

    [*A second knock is heard, louder than the
      first.*

Mrs. Willoughby : "There's a knock.
[*She rises.*] Perhaps it's Captain Strong—
I mean Major Strong—and I'm sure my hair
is coming down. [*She runs to the door of
her own room, and then says*] : Come in !"

IV

[*The door opens, and* Dr. Doulton *enters.*

Dr. Doulton: "Good-evening."

Mrs. Willoughby (*coming forward again*) : "Oh, it's only you?"

Dr. Doulton : "Only I? Pray, whom were you expecting? The President of the United States or the Czar of Russia?"

[*He glances quickly about the room.*

Mrs. Willoughby: "The czar is not more autocratic than a family physician."

Dr. Doulton : "Your family physician will not condemn you to the knout this evening—though you probably deserve it."

Mrs. Willoughby : "Why?"

Dr. Doulton: "Because you are a woman, and a woman spends half her time in making mischief and the other half trying to hide it. The world would come to an end very soon if it were not that she is her own worst enemy, and hurts herself twice as much as any one else. [*Looking at her carefully.*] What have you been up to now ?"

Mrs. Willoughby (*uncomfortably*): "Don't stare at one like that."

Dr. Doulton: "You have been getting angry—that's what you have been doing."

Mrs. Willoughby (*surprised*): "How did you know ?"

Dr. Doulton: "A little bird told me—or a pair of them, rather—the two robin-red-breasts which flamed in your cheeks just now."

Mrs. Willoughby (*running to the mirror over the mantel-piece*): "Am I red ? I hate to have too much color."

Dr. Doulton (*taking a chair*): "That's because you are a woman, and therefore un-reasonable."

Mrs. Willoughby : "You are a Russian to-night—a regular bear."

Dr. Doulton: "I am. [*He holds out his hand.*] And here's my paw. Let me have yours."

[*She extends her arm and he feels her pulse.*

Mrs. Willoughby (*after a pause*): "Well?"

Dr. Doulton: "What did the woman write to make you so angry?"

Mrs. Willoughby (*hotly*): "She was insufferable! [*Suddenly.*] But how did you know anything about her?"

Dr. Doulton: "I put two and two together—the flush on your cheeks; this letter you have received here [*indicating envelope on the table*] and that one you have been writing there" [*indicating desk*].

Mrs. Willoughby: "Sometimes I am afraid of you."

Dr. Doulton: "People generally are afraid of doctors and lawyers, and that's why they abuse us and fear us. A man can have few secrets that his counsel or his physician can't know—and a woman hasn't any."

Mrs. Willoughby: "Then perhaps you can tell me what is the matter with me lately?"

Dr. Doulton: "Just now you are excited, partly because you have been writing an angry letter, and partly because our good friend, Major Strong, is going to leave us to-night on his way to the front again."

Mrs. Willoughby (*taking up a paper-cutter from the table*): "Of course we shall all miss him."

Dr. Doulton: "Of course. Those are pretty flowers he has sent you."

Mrs. Willoughby (*surprised again*): "Well, you are the—"

Dr. Doulton: "No; I'm not the devil—but you left his card by the side of the vase."

Mrs. Willoughby (*laughing*): "You seem to see everything. There is something un-canny about you."

[*She drops the paper-cutter.*

Dr. Doulton: "You are restless. You

MRS. WILLOUGHBY

have been laughing with me, but you have been crying nearly all the afternoon.

[Mrs. Willoughby *turns away from him.*

Dr. Doulton : "If you don't control yourself, you will cry again now, and I shall have a case of hysteria on my hands."

Mrs. Willoughby (*taking her handkerchief from her eyes*) : "I am not going to give way again, doctor, but I confess I have been feeling strangely all day. I don't know what is the matter."

Dr. Doulton : "I do."

Mrs. Willoughby : "What is it ?"

Dr. Doulton : "They call me blunt because sometimes I say sharp things. That may sound like a paradox, but it isn't. Now, if I tell you the medicine you need, two things will happen : you won't take it—and you won't thank me."

Mrs. Willoughby : "Indeed I shall, doctor. I will do whatever you bid me. I will take anything you prescribe."

Dr. Doulton : "Sure ?"

Mrs. Willoughby : "Try me."

Dr. Doulton : "**I will.**"

Mrs. Willoughby (*anxiously*) : " Is my mal-
ady so very serious, then ?"

Dr. Doulton: "No, your complaint is com-
mon enough. You are suffering from idle-
ness and from lack of something to think
about—or, I should say, for lack of somebody
to think about."

Mrs. Willoughby : " I am not sure that **I**
understand you."

Dr. Doulton : " **Yes,** you are—if you **will**
pardon my frankness—you are a young
woman, and it is not good **for** woman to be
alone. You need something to occupy **your**
mind. Marry !"

Mrs. Willoughby : "Doctor !"

Dr. Doulton : "Of all the ill weeds which
grow apace, the most useless and pernicious
are those worn by **a** widow. [*He touches
the flowers on the table before him.*] Plant
these forget-me-nots on his grave, if you
will, and **strew** these lilies **of** the valley

above him, if you like ; but remember that you are young yet, and that there are roses in the world still."

Mrs. Willoughby : " They are not for me."

Dr. Doulton : " Why not?"

Mrs. Willoughby: " Why not? Because I am loyal to the dead!"

Dr. Doulton: " As your medical adviser, I don't mind telling you that that's a poor reason."

Mrs. Willoughby (*hastily*): "It must suffice."

Dr. Doulton: "But it doesn't. I hold that matrimony is like law—if you lose your first case, you must move for a retrial."

Mrs. Willoughby: " Ah, doctor, haven't I had trials enough? Come, come, let us change the subject."

Dr. Doulton : " That's just what I have been suggesting. If you will change the subject of your thoughts, and, above all, of your emotions, I think I can guarantee a cure."

4

Mrs. Willoughby: "But I refuse to take the medicine."

Dr. Doulton : "Then I'm afraid I must give up the case."

Mrs. Willoughby: "You had better give up the attempt to make me alter my resolve. I am as fixed as Penelope."

Dr. Doulton : "But although her husband told travellers' tales and could draw the long-bow, he was at least alive."

Mrs. Willoughby (*with reserve, and after a marked pause*): "It has been very warm to-day for so early in the spring; don't you think so, doctor ?"

Dr. Doulton: "I think that I had better retire in good order, while a way of retreat is left open to me."

Mrs. Willoughby: "So do I."

Dr. Doulton : "But I do not give up. In matrimony as in medicine, while there's life there's hope."

Mrs. Willoughby: "You need not fear that I shall make a death-bed recantation."

[*A knock is heard at the door of the parlor.*

Mrs. Willoughby : "I do believe that's Major Strong! [*Running to the door of her own room.*] And I have been so upset by my talk with you that I must look like a fright! I shall leave you to entertain him! Come in!"

V

[*As the parlor door opens and* **Major Strong** *enters,* Mrs. Willoughby *disappears into her own room on one side. The* Major *is in uniform. He comes forward.*

Major Strong : "**Ah**, doctor, **isn't Mrs.** Willoughby here?"

Mrs. Willoughby (*behind the door of her room*) : " Take a chair. Major, and talk to the doctor.   **I** shall be with you in a minute!"

Dr. Doulton (*in disgust*) : "**Now**, isn't that like **a** woman?   She runs away to arrange **her** masked batteries **when** she hears you come—"

Major Strong : "Indeed?"

Dr. Doulton : " Quite regardless of the fact that she has been talking to me calmly for ten minutes."

Major Strong : " But you are a doctor."

Dr. Doulton : " But I'm a man, am I not ? There's really no need of these women-doctors they say they want ; they don't think of us as men now. They treat us as automatic, pulse-feeling, and pill-distributing waxworks."

Major Strong : " You had better have stayed in the army."

Dr. Doulton : " So I am beginning to think."

Major Strong : " You were intended by nature for a military surgeon — you take so much delight in cutting up your friends."

Dr. Doulton (*turning on him*): " It's a pity you didn't fall into my hands when that bullet hit you in the shoulder. [*With a sudden return of kindliness.*] How is the pain in the arm, eh?"

Major Strong : " Almost gone."

Dr. Doulton : " I can give you some little pills for it, if you like."

Major Strong : " It was a little pill of lead that gave it to me, but I saw the gentleman who prescribed it, and I took a leaf out of your book—like cures like, you know—and I cured him of the fever of living."

Dr. Doulton: "I don't think you are well enough yet to go back to the army; dining on salt-horse and boiled rye and sleeping in a rifle-pit will not help that shoulder to heal."

Major Strong (*quietly*): "We are going forward to-night."

Dr. Doulton : "I don't advise you to go."

Major Strong : "You speak as my physician?"

Dr. Doulton : "Of course."

Major Strong : "But as my friend, you wouldn't have me lag behind while the regiment went to the front, would you?"

Dr. Doulton : "There's no use talking to you boys in blue; you are color-blind just now—you see red. You soldiers all want to go out and kill somebody."

Major Strong : "We can't all be doctors, you know."

Dr. Doulton: "Now I'm a homœopath and a man of peace—"

Major Strong: "Yet you served three years."

Dr. Doulton: "I was carried away by all your talk of blood and iron, and I went forth with fire and sword. Now I have experienced a change of heart, and I prescribe bread pills for old maids' poodles."

Major Strong: "That is to say, you wish you were going with us to-night?"

Dr. Doulton: "Of course I do. When do you start?"

Major Strong: "In an hour or so, I suppose. You know I have been appointed to a new regiment from the western part of the State. It is on its way from Albany now. I believe the Seventh is going up to the station to escort it down to the ferry. It is only by special favor that I have been allowed to remain here all winter trying to get well; but as the boys pass down Fifth Avenue this evening I am to join them.

We take the cars for Washington to-night, and—"

Dr. Doulton : "And to-morrow you will be sent forward to the Army of the Potomac."

Major Strong : "And we shall soon start on our usual summer excursion, 'On to Richmond.' Hitherto we have always failed to make the connections, but there's a new time-table this year and a new conductor, and we hope to get through by daylight."

Dr. Doulton (*impatiently*) : " Don't talk to me about it, or I shall be tempted to murder you, steal your uniform, and take your place."

Major Strong : "I've no doubt there will be many a day when I shall wish you had."

Dr. Doulton (*watching him*) : " Mrs. Willoughby will miss you."

Major Strong : "I hope she will."

Dr. Doulton : "And you will miss her?"

Major Strong : "I am sure I shall."

Dr. Doulton : "She's a charming woman

—isn't she?--with a fine figure, and a pretty foot, and a—"

Major Strong (*with reserve*): "She is a woman whose charms I am not willing to discuss even with you, doctor."

Dr. Doulton: "And you are quite right, too. Never pick a woman to pieces. Women are like religion: you've got to take them on faith; if you go to probing and analyzing, you turn out a sceptic—and you don't fall in love."

Major Strong: "Doctor—"

Dr. Doulton: "Come, come, you cannot deny that you soldiers fall in love as easily as you fall in line—and almost as often."

Major Strong: "I have been in love but once in my life."

Dr. Doulton: "I make a habit of falling in love once a year. I prescribe it to myself. I find it a most valuable specific against old age."

Major Strong: "If you could only patent the remedy, you might make your fortune."

5

Dr. Doulton: "And that reminds me—I hear Mrs. Willoughby is very rich."

Major Strong (*carelessly*): "Yes? [*Earnestly.*] But rich or poor, the man who gains her will get a treasure beyond all price."

Dr. Doulton: "Of course. And she says she will never marry again. Yet, then, all young widows say that, and very few of them keep their word. She's a clever woman, a little light-headed, perhaps, but naturally light-hearted. Just now she is mourning her husband, and she is mourning more than is necessary; probably out of remorse that she did not love him enough when he was alive."

Major Strong (*quickly*): "What makes you think that?"

Dr. Doulton: "Knowledge of the sex, that's all. By-the-way, do you happen to know whether her husband was the dashing Dick Willoughby who was killed in New Orleans?"

Major Strong (*starting*): "Why ?"

Dr. Doulton: "Oh, no matter. I knew *him* pretty well — Dashing Dick Willoughby of the Fighting Forty-first, as they used to call him. A good soldier he was, too, a happy-go-lucky, devil-may-care fellow, easy-going and hard-living. Curious, wasn't it, that after risking himself recklessly, running the gantlet of a dozen pitched battles, always ready to lead a forlorn hope, he should have been shot at last by a woman?"

Major Strong: "A woman?"

Dr. Doulton: "And she was a very pretty girl, indeed, a black-haired, black-eyed beauty—a Cuban, I fancy. He had brought her with him to New Orleans, and there he took up with another woman. Then the first girl shot him—almost through the heart: a most beautiful case it was; he didn't live two hours."

Major Strong: "I've heard of this Dick Willoughby, but I thought he was killed in battle, or just after, by a rebel?"

Dr. Doulton: "Well, the girl was a rebel, I suppose."

Major Strong: "Isn't this all idle gossip?"

Dr. Doulton: "It is solid fact."

Major Strong: "How do you know?"

Dr. Doulton: "I was the surgeon who attended him when he died. [*After a pause.*] He left a wife, I believe—at least, I think I heard he had married some pretty little girl from up country somewhere—"

Major Strong: "Poor woman!"

Dr. Doulton: "I believe she had money, too; that's the kind of woman he would want for a wife — rich enough to let him spend freely and innocent enough to ask no questions. He used to say that women were like pease: they were best when they were young and tender—and green."

Major Strong: "And this is the fellow she may be mourning over to this day?"

Dr. Doulton: "Of course."

Major Strong: "Poor woman!"

Dr. Doulton (*looking at his watch*): "But

"HE TOOK UP WITH ANOTHER WOMAN"

I can't stay here chatting with you all night.
I have letters which must be written this
evening. As Mrs. Willoughby evidently
doesn't intend to return while I am here, I
shall leave the coast clear for her. I'll come
back before you go."

[Dr. Doulton *walks out briskly, banging
the door after him.*

VI

Major Strong (*looking after the* Doctor): "He's a queer customer, but shrewd, too— as keen as one of his own scalpels. How sharply he saw into that Dick Willoughby! I wonder if that fellow was a relative of hers? [*Starting.*] Could he have been her husband? I think I once heard her say that her husband had died at New Orleans. And yet it is impossible! No man married to her could ever have looked at another woman. I love her!—oh, how I love her!—and I must know my fate now. I have put it off day after day. And if she refuses me — why, then, it is lucky we are ordered to the front. [*He takes up her photograph from table.*] How beautiful she is! They say that every lover lends his mistress a magic mantle that hides her defects and magnifies her charms; but she has no need of any such, for no painter could do her justice, and even the cruel sun cannot take from her beauty."

VII

[Mrs. Willoughby *enters quietly from her room and stands on one side of the parlor, watching* Major Strong.

Major Strong: "My love!"

[*He kisses the photograph.*

Mrs. Willoughby: "Well—"

Major Strong (*turning in astonishment*): "Oh!"

Mrs. Willoughby: "What are you doing?"

Major Strong (*confused*): "What was I doing?"

Mrs. Willoughby (*coming forward*): "Yes. What were you doing with that photograph?"

Major Strong: "That photograph?"

Mrs. Willoughby: "Yes? That photograph?"

Major Strong (*recovering himself*): "I

thought it was a speaking likeness and I was whispering to it, to try if it would answer me."

Mrs. Willoughby: "And what were you whispering?"

Major Strong (*boldly*): "It is your portrait, and I was telling it that I—I—"

[*Catching* Mrs. Willoughby's *eye, he stops abruptly.*

Mrs. Willoughby: "You were telling it—what? Go on!"

Major Strong (*in confusion again*): "I was telling it a secret—which I may tell you—some day."

Mrs. Willoughby (*sitting on the sofa*): "Then I'm sorry I was not able to surprise you a minute sooner; perhaps I should have overheard it then. They say listeners never hear any good of themselves; and I'm certain they never hear it of anybody else."

Major Strong (*taking a chair by her side*): "Surely, you have never caught any one speaking ill of you?"

6

Mrs. Willoughby: "Oh yes — often ; in fact, whenever I talk to myself."

Major Strong (*smiling*): "Then you have one detractor more than I thought, and one against whom I cannot defend you. Of what do you accuse yourself?"

Mrs. Willoughby: "Of rudeness—in keeping you waiting so long; and of barbarity, in exposing you to the tender mercies of that raging lion, the doctor; and of forgetfulness, too — for I have not yet thanked you for these lovely flowers. [*She rises and goes to the table.*] They are exquisite! How did you guess that these were my favorites?"

Major Strong: "I heard you say once that roses and lilies of the valley were the flowers you liked best, and I ventured to add a few forget-me-nots, because I shall hope that you will keep a place in your memory for me when I go away—"

Mrs. Willoughby (*musing*): "I remember I carried a bunch of lilies of the valley at my wedding. Dick had given them to me."

Major Strong (*startled*): "Dick?"

Mrs. Willoughby: "My husband—Colonel Willoughby."

Major Strong: "Was Colonel Willoughby's name Richard?"

Mrs. Willoughby: "Yes. They used to call him Dashing Dick Willoughby, and they said he was the idol of the Fighting Forty-first."

Major Strong: "Ah!"

Mrs. Willoughby: "I was not fit to be the wife of such a hero; I was but a silly school-girl, and I have often wondered how he had patience with me. But he had always a bright smile and a pleasant word for me whenever I was with him. He was so popular, and there were so many demands on his time, that I saw very little of him. Why, the very winter we were married, he had to go down to Cuba all alone to attend to some business for a dear friend."

Major Strong: "So he went to Cuba?"

Mrs. Willoughby: "Yes; and he had scarcely been home a fortnight before the war broke out, and of course he volunteered at once, and I never saw him again."

[*And here she hides her face in handkerchief.*

Major Strong: "And he was shot at the taking of New Orleans?"

Mrs. Willoughby (*fiercely*): "He was murdered by some rebel after the city had surrendered."

Major Strong: "Murdered?"

Mrs. Willoughby: "I cannot tell you any details of his death, because my father said they were too painful for me, and he would not let me read the papers for a month or more."

Major Strong: "Your father was very considerate."

Mrs. Willoughby (*suddenly*): "Do you believe that soldiers are always falling in love?"

Major Strong: "I know one soldier at least who has fallen in love but once in his life— for the first time and the last."

Mrs. Willoughby (*looking at him*): "Tell me about him. I dote on love-stories."

Major Strong (*quailing under her glance*): "Well—well—I should like to tell you, but—"

Mrs. Willoughby: "But?"

Major Strong (*confused*): "But I cannot recollect all the circumstances just now."

Mrs. Willoughby: "Perhaps you may recall them later."

Major Strong: "Perhaps—perhaps."

[*There is a pause for a little space.*

Mrs. Willoughby: "Charming weather we are having for so early in the spring."

Major Strong (*taking courage*): "Charming, indeed."

Mrs. Willoughby: "Such a pleasant change after this most disagreeable winter. We have had nothing but snow and ice, rain and thaw —a most exasperating alternation of snow-heaps and mud-puddles."

Major Strong: "I had not noticed it. I thought it was the most delightful winter I had ever known."

Mrs. Willoughby : "Then you must have kept in-doors."

Major Strong : "No, I have taken many a long walk; but, then, I was not thinking of the weather; my mind was full of something else."

Mrs. Willoughby : "If it kept you from discovering what an unbearable winter we are having, it must have been something very agreeable."

Major Strong : "It was."

[*There is another pause.*

Mrs. Willoughby : "I suppose you are sorry to have to give up the gayety of New York."

Major Strong : "I have pleasant memories to take with me."

Mrs. Willoughby : "Some of the balls this winter were really very pretty, and quite worth remembering."

Major Strong : "There is one of them I can never forget—the one at which I first met you."

Mrs. Willoughby : "That was only a little party!"

Major Strong : "It seemed like a glimpse of heaven to a man who has been in a military hospital for six months."

Mrs. Willoughby : " I remember that you looked very pale and weak."

Major Strong : "And I remember that you looked so beautiful, so gracious, so good! My eyes followed you about the room until I was afraid you must have discovered it."

Mrs. Willoughby : "I did."

Major Strong (*taken aback*): "Oh!"

Mrs. Willoughby : " I thought you were a most interesting invalid, and I asked who you were. Just as one friend told me that you were Captain Strong, wounded in the shoulder at Gettysburg in the repulse of Pickett's charge, another friend came up and asked permission to present you."

Major Strong : " You wore a black dress like the one you wear now; and you had a bunch of red roses and lilies of the valley. You were very kind to me then, as you have been always. You gave me a rose."

Mrs. Willoughby : "Did I?"

Major Strong : "Would you like to see it ?"

Mrs. Willoughby : "You don't mean to say that you have saved up a few withered rose leaves?"

Major Strong : "Yes."

Mrs. Willoughby (*gently*): "How foolish of you!"

Major Strong (*earnestly*) : "I have two relics which I keep together—the rose which you gave me and the bullet the surgeon cut out of my shoulder six months earlier. I was very ill when I came on here to New York, and the doctors did not know what was the matter with me or why I did not get well. When I first saw you I was wellnigh sick unto death. I had kept the bullet that had almost killed me, and when I went home from that party I took it out and put it with the rose you had given me—the rose which brought me back to life. And I have treasured them ever since — the bane and antidote."

Mrs. Willoughby (*moved in spite of herself*): "How much you make of a trifle! [*She hesitates for a moment.*] And so you go tonight?"

Major Strong : "In less than an hour."

   [*The sound of an approaching band begins to be audible.*

Mrs. Willoughby: "So soon?"

Major Strong (*encouraged*): "My time is short, you see; and if I have anything to say before I go, I must say it promptly. And I have something to say—something of the utmost importance to me—"

Mrs. Willoughby (*starting up*): "There are soldiers now! I hear the band. [*She goes to the window.*] Surely this is not your regiment yet?"

Major Strong: "It is the Seventh, going to escort us from the station to the ferry."

7

[*The band passes under the windows playing " Tramp, Tramp, Tramp, the Boys
are Marching.*"

Mrs. Willoughby: " I confess I shall miss
you. We have been good friends all winter."

Major Strong (*earnestly*): " Can I not hope
that I may be more than a friend?"

Mrs. Willoughby: " Major Strong—"

Major Strong: "I have made the plunge
and must go on now while I have the courage. Do not interrupt me. Hear me out.
You must have seen that I love you! I have
not dared to speak until now when I have
only a few minutes left me. But you cannot have been blind to my devotion. I have
waited on your words; I have been ready
to follow you like a dumb dog. I love
you!"

[*The music of the band begins to die away
in the distance.*

Mrs. Willoughby: " I am very sorry, but—"

Major Strong (*impetuously*): " I tried to tell
you this once before, but you would not listen

to me. Do not say me no. If you cannot love me now, at least let me hope that I may win you in time."

Mrs. Willoughby · "Do not think me hard, if—"

Major Strong: "I could not think you any·thing but perfect. All you do is well done—even though I may be the sufferer."

Mrs. Willoughby: "The love of an honest man is a thing no woman may put aside lightly; it is an honor she cannot but feel; it raises her in her own esteem. But—"

Major Strong: "But you do not love me now? Then give me time to try to win you. I will love you so much that you cannot but love me a little."

Mrs. Willoughby: "I will not say that you are indifferent to me. Your friendship is precious, and I have taken pleasure in being with you."

Major Strong (*seizing her hand*): "Then I may hope?"

Mrs. Willoughby (*withdrawing her hand*):

"Perhaps, under other circumstances, I would not bid you despair—"

Major Strong (*quickly*): "That is all I ask."

Mrs. Willoughby: "And it is more than I can grant, as it is. I do not hold myself free to love and to marry."

Major Strong: "Why not?"

Mrs. Willoughby: "I have a husband."

Major Strong: "But he is dead!"

Mrs. Willoughby: "The dead are never dead till we forget!"

Major Strong: "Then you refuse me because you wish to be faithful to your husband's memory?"

Mrs. Willoughby: "I don't think I said that exactly—did I?"

Major Strong: "Perhaps you did not say it in so many words."

Mrs. Willoughby: "I thought not."

Major Strong: "Would you hold yourself released if your husband had been unfaithful to you?"

Mrs. Willoughby (*fiercely rising*): "Major Strong, such a suggestion is wholly unworthy of you! I do not think it becoming in an officer and a gentleman to insult one who is not here to defend himself."

Major Strong (*with dignity*): "If I knew that the only way to win you was to break down your faith in your husband, I could not do it, much as I love you."

Mrs. Willoughby (*holding out her hand to him*): "There spoke the true man again—the real friend. [Major Strong *kisses her hand.*] We shall always be friends, I trust. I cannot be your wife — but I will be your sister, if you like."

Major Strong: "I must make the best of what I can; and though sister is a cold word to one as much in love as I am, yet I seize it gratefully, for it tells me that you do not dislike me, and that you are willing to let me love you."

Mrs. Willoughby: "You may love me as a sister."

Major Strong: "Then you must call me John."

Mrs. Willoughby: "Must I?"

Major Strong: "A sister usually calls her brother by his given name, doesn't she?"

Mrs. Willoughby: "I suppose so."

Major Strong: "And I must call you—Mary."

Mrs. Willoughby: "But only when we are alone together."

Major Strong (*eagerly*): "And when I get back from the war, we shall be alone together as much as possible—eh, Sister Mary?"

[*He kisses her.*

Mrs. Willoughby (*indignantly*): "Major Strong!"

Major Strong: "Is not a brother allowed to kiss his sister?"

Mrs. Willoughby: "Certainly not."

Major Strong (*penitently*): "I had thought it was customary."

Mrs. Willoughby: "This is carrying a jest a little too far, Maj—"

Major Strong (*prompting her*): "John — Sister Mary."

Mrs. Willoughby (*smiling again*): "But I will forgive you, John, if it doesn't occur again."

Major Strong (*taking her hand*): "I may kiss your hand?"

Mrs. Willoughby: "I don't know whether I ought to let you do that or not."

Major Strong: "Then I will decide for you."   [*He kisses her hand.*

Mrs. Willoughby: "Do you think a brother would want to kiss his sister's hand?"

Major Strong (*passionately*): "I don't know what a brother would do! I know only that I should like to keep this hand forever."

[*He kisses it again tenderly.*

Mrs. Willoughby (*withdrawing her hand*): "That is not the way a brother talks."

Major Strong: "I can't help it! I must—"

Mrs. Willoughby: "Now, don't let us have this unpleasant scene over again! If you want us to be friends, you must not speak again about what can never be."

Major Strong: "I shall try to please you, but—"

[*A knock is heard.*

Mrs. Willoughby: "Come in."

VIII

[The hall-boy *enters.*

The hall-boy: "I've found the picture at last, mum."

Mrs. Willoughby: "Where was it ?"

The hall-boy: "It was in the bar-room, mum. Two old soldiers saw it in the hall, and they knew it for Colonel Willoughby at once, for they had been in his regiment."

Mrs. Willoughby (*eagerly*): "Well ?"

The hall-boy: "They said it looked as natural as life—so they took it up to the bar and offered it a drink."

Mrs. Willoughby (*to* Major Strong): "You see how his men all loved him!"

Major Strong: "Yes, I see."

Mrs. Willoughby (*to the* hall-boy): "Where is the picture now ?"

The hall-boy: "I've got it outside here."

8

Mrs. Willoughby: "Bring it in at once."

The hall-boy: "All right, mum. [*Going toward the door, he pauses before* Major Strong.] I heard them say in the office, Major, that your bill was all ready, as you had asked for it, and all your things are out of your room now." [*He goes out.*

Major Strong (*moving toward the door*):
"I will run down for a minute and settle
everything."

Mrs. Willoughby: "It is true, then, that
you are going to-night?"

Major Strong: "In a few minutes the regiment will be down here, and I must fall in
and march away. May I come back and say
good-bye ?"

Mrs. Willoughby: "I should never forgive
you if you did not. Let me have the last
word with you—it is a woman's privilege to
have the last word, you know. Maj—"

Major Strong (*interrupting her*): "John—
Sister Mary."

[*He kisses her hand and goes out, leaving
the door open.*

Mrs. Willoughby (*looking after him*): "I feel proud to be loved by such a man. And how handsome he looks in his uniform! If it was not that my heart is buried in the grave—I don't know but that I might—perhaps—"

> [*The* hall-boy *appears at the door with a large painting.*

Mrs. Willoughby: "Is that it?"

The hall-boy: "Yes, mum."

Mrs. Willoughby: "Put it on this easel here."

The hall-boy (*placing the picture on the easel*): "It looks just like the Colonel, don't it, mum? I don't wonder the boys asked it to take something."

Mrs. Willoughby (*stiffly*): "That will do."

The hall-boy (*going to the door*): "You see

I used to know the colonel, mum, before the war. He was a gay old boy, I can tell you!"

Mrs. Willoughby (*sharply*): "You may go now."

The hall-boy: "All right, mum."

[*He leaves the room through the open door. Mrs. Willoughby, standing silently before the picture, sighs, and begins to drape an American flag over the top of the easel.*

Mrs. Willoughby: "It is very like him. This is really Dashing Dick Willoughby, of the Fighting Forty-first; and I can gaze on it without tears. How is it, I wonder?"

XI

Dr. Doulton (*appears at the door, saying*): "Strong hasn't gone yet ?"

Mrs. Willoughby: "Not yet. But he has to go in a few minutes."

Dr. Doulton (*taking a chair*): "I will try to get back before he is off."

Mrs. Willoughby: "Why not wait here now?"

Dr. Doulton: "I can't. My professional services are required elsewhere in the hotel."

Mrs. Willoughby: "Is anybody ill ?"

Dr. Doulton: "There is another widow in the house, and she has something to occupy her mind. It is a cat, and it has been ailing for a day or two; and now I have just been summoned to attend it."

Mrs. Willoughby: "Then you must hurry

back again, for I expect to hear the band every minute."

> [*She finishes draping the flag over the top of the picture-frame, and she moves back from the easel, looking at it.*

Dr. Doulton (*seeing picture*) : "What's this?"

Mrs. Willoughby : "A picture, as you see."

Dr. Doulton : "Are you starting a gallery?"

Mrs. Willoughby: "It is a portrait of my husband."

Dr. Doulton (*crossing over to the picture and reading the inscription on the frame*): "'Colonel Richard Willoughby, U. S. V., treacherously killed by a rebel at New Orleans after the surrender of the city. Presented to the New York Historical Society by his devoted widow.' Oh, ho! So you *are* the devoted widow of Dashing Dick Willoughby, of the Fighting Forty-first?"

Mrs. Willoughby: "Yes."

Dr. Doulton (*dryly*): " Ah! I thought so. [*He looks at her keenly.*] Then I can give you news of your husband."

Mrs. Willoughby (*starting*): "You don't mean to say that—that— [*Quickly*]: He isn't *alive*, is he?"

Dr. Doulton (*grimly*): "No, he's dead. I saw to that! I attended him myself."

Mrs. Willoughby (*dropping into a chair*): "You did startle me so!"

Dr. Doulton: "I meant it!"

Mrs. Willoughby; "Why?"

Dr. Doulton: "Everybody underestimates the therapeutic advantages of startling a widow who is mourning over an unworthy husband."

Mrs. Willoughby (*rising quickly*): "Doctor Doulton!"

Dr. Doulton (*brusquely*): "You do not propose to water his grave with your tears all your life, do you?"

Mrs. Willoughby (*with dignity*): "Yes."

Dr. Doulton: "He wasn't worth it."

Mrs. Willoughby (*severely*): " I cannot permit—"

Dr. Doulton: " He wasn't worth a single tear from you."

Mrs. Willoughby: "Doctor, I will not allow—"

Dr. Doulton (*going to the table and pouring out a glass of water*): "Take a little sip."

Mrs. Willoughby (*taking the glass*): " If you have any bad news, tell me quickly."

Dr. Doulton (*feeling her pulse*): "I will."

Mrs. Willoughby (*tearfully*): " I can stand it."

[*She sets down the glass of water untasted.*

Dr. Doulton: "I am sure you can."

Mrs. Willoughby (*anxiously*): " Go on, doctor, *do* go on! Don't you see that I am all on fire ?"

Dr. Doulton: " I see that—and I see, too, that you are ready to believe what I tell you. It's no more than the truth. I knew Dick Willoughby well. He was a good-for-noth-

9

ing and a ne'er-do-well. He drank and he gambled."

Mrs. Willoughby: "It is cowardly of you to accuse him now."

Dr. Doulton: "He was a spendthrift and a fortune-hunter; probably he married you for your money."

Mrs. Willoughby: "Do you think I will believe this?"

Dr. Doulton: "He was a libertine, and he was shot by a woman whom he had brought with him and abandoned for another."

Mrs. Willoughby: "It isn't true! It can't be true!"

Dr. Doulton: "I was with him when he died; and I saw the body of the poor wretch who had killed him."

Mrs. Willoughby: "Was she hanged?"

Dr. Doulton: "She took poison five minutes after your husband died."

Mrs. Willoughby (*falling back on the sofa*): "This is too horrible!"

Dr. Doulton: "You are like the rest. A

woman refuses to see the clay feet of her idol until it is humbled in the dust before her."

Mrs. Willoughby: "I won't believe it! There must be some mistake."

Dr. Doulton: "You are even harder to convince than Major Strong."

Mrs. Willoughby (*surprised*): "He doesn't know of this?"

Dr. Doulton: "I told him."

Mrs. Willoughby: "You told him? When?"

"Dr. Doulton: "This evening — not an hour ago—while we were waiting for you."

Mrs. Willoughby: "And he never said a word to me!"

Dr. Doulton: "He couldn't tell you, of course; he's a soldier; I'm a doctor; and we use fire and sword in different ways. My weapons are the bistoury and the scalpel, and as I saw that your love for your husband was morbid, I cut it out and cauterized the wound."

Mrs. Willoughby: "He knew, and he never said a word."

Dr. Doulton: "Honesty forbade his yielding to the temptation — though it may not console him for the consequences of having resisted. But I cannot dally here any longer. I must go to my patient—the invalid cat of the other widow. [*He turns to the door.*] Don't let the Major go till I say good-bye to him."

Mrs. Willoughby (*impatiently*): "Yes— yes."

XII

[Dr. Doulton *goes out, leaving the door open behind him.* Mrs. Willoughby *stands silent in thought for a moment or two. Then she comes forward and drops the flag across the portrait so as to hide the face.*

Mrs. Willoughby: "But it is best always to learn the truth."

[Major Strong *appears in the doorway; he has put on his belt and his sword, and his cap is in his hand.*

Major Strong : "May I come in?"

Mrs. Willoughby (*feverishly excited*): "Oh —yes—you may come in!"

Major Strong : "I have only a minute or two more ; the boys are very near here now."

Mrs. Willoughby: " And you must go?"

Major Strong (*surprised*): "Certainly."

Mrs. Willoughby: "Even if I asked you to stay?"

Major Strong: "I am under orders."

Mrs. Willoughby (*enthusiastically*): "Ah, that is noble! That is like you — always ready to do your duty!"

Major Strong (*surprised again*): "I hope so."

Mrs. Willoughby: "Do you think that I do not see your heroism, and that I do not thank you for it? I understand you at last!"

Major Strong: "I do not know that I quite understand you now."

Mrs. Willoughby: "I thank you, and I look up to you!"

Major Strong: "You are excited, I see."

Mrs. Willoughby: "Excited? And well I may be!"

Major Strong (*alarmed*): "Are you ill?"

Mrs. Willoughby: "No; I am well, at last."

Major Strong: "You are nervous. Shall I send for Dr. Doulton?"

Mrs. Willoughby: "I have just seen him."

Major Strong (*anxiously*): "And what did he say?"

Mrs. Willoughby: "He told me of your goodness and of his baseness."

Major Strong (*puzzled*): "The doctor's baseness?"

Mrs. Willoughby: "No, of my husband's."

> [*The music of an approaching band is heard, playing "Johnny Comes Marching Home."*

Major Strong: "What did he tell you?"

Mrs. Willoughby: "He told me how my husband died, and who killed him."

Major Strong (*hotly*): "Then he took a most unwarrantable liberty—"

Mrs. Willoughby: "And he did me a most inestimable service."

> [*The band has come nearer and nearer; it is now almost under the window.*

Major Strong: "There is my regiment!"

Mrs. Willoughby: "Must you go at once?"

Major Strong: "I have no choice."

Mrs. Willoughby: "Without one word?"

Major Strong: "What can I say that I have not said already? You will not let me tell I love you."

Mrs. Willoughby: "Won't I?"

Major Strong: "You told me not to speak of it again."

Mrs. Willoughby: "Did I?"

Major Strong: "What can I do but obey?"

Mrs. Willoughby: "That's just like a man! You go on in your straightforward way—and—and you never see things—"

Major Strong: "You have rejected me twice already."

Mrs. Willoughby: "Didn't they teach you at school that two negatives make an affirmative?"

Major Strong (*joyfully*): "Do you mean to hint that I may hope?"

[Mrs. Willoughby *stands silent for a moment. Then* Major Strong *starts forward, clasps her in his arms and kisses her.*

Major Strong: "Then you will take me at last, Mary?"

Mrs. Willoughby: "If you will take me, John."

Major Strong: "Then we are engaged?"

Mrs. Willoughby: "I suppose so."

Major Strong: "When will you marry me?"

Mrs. Willoughby: "How impatient the man is. Why, we are only just engaged, and you want me to name the day."

Major Strong: "When can we be married?"

Mrs. Willoughby: "You asked me that before."

Major Strong: "And you must give me an answer quickly, for I must be off at once."

Mrs. Willoughby (*clinging to him*): "I cannot bear to let you go now — but I must — I know I must. And I will try to bear myself bravely, as becomes a soldier's wife."

Major Strong: "And when will you be his wife?"

10

Mrs. Willoughby: "Come back to me and I will marry you whenever you please."

Major Strong: "My darling!"

XIII

[*As he embraces her* Dr. Doulton *appears in the doorway.*

[*When the* doctor *sees* Mrs. Willoughby *in* Major Strong's *arms he starts back.*

Dr. Doulton: "Oh! and I meant to marry her myself!"